THERE'S A TIGER IN THE GARDEN

LIZZY STEWART

Frances Lincoln
Children's Books

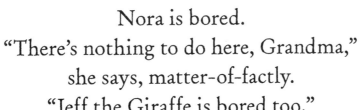

Nora is bored.
"There's nothing to do here, Grandma,"
she says, matter-of-factly.
"Jeff the Giraffe is bored too."

"Why don't you play in the garden?" says Nora's grandma. "I thought I saw a tiger there earlier."

"A tiger?" asks Nora. "There's no tiger in the garden. I'm too old for silly games!"
"I'm sure I saw one..." she replies.

"And dragonflies the size of birds and plants
that can swallow you up whole! And a polar bear
who likes fishing, though he's a bit grumpy.
But most magnificent of all was the tiger.

You and Jeff should take a look . . .
If you don't believe me."

"She's being silly, Jeff,"
says Nora, standing
outside in the garden.

"There's no tiger here.
Just the same boring old
garden, with boring old
plants and boring old…"

Whoosh!

Something whizzes past Nora's face.

It's a
dragonfly!

"Wow!" says Nora.

"**Well,**" Nora says to Jeff, "there might be dragonflies as big as birds but I know, for a fact, that there aren't plants that'll eat us whole, or a grumpy polar bear and there's definitely no tiger."

"Come on Jeff, let's go home."

"Fine.

So there ARE dragonflies the size of birds, and that bush definitely wanted to eat you, BUT I don't see any polar bear and there's no sign of this ridiculous tiger anywhere."

"Come on Jeff, let's go home."

"Hello," says a gruff, grizzly voice.

"Oh! Uh... Hello,"
replies Nora.

"I suppose you're looking for that wretched
tiger, aren't you? Hmmph," says the
polar bear. "No one ever comes
looking for ME."

"Oh, not you as well!" shouts Nora.

"There is NO tiger living in my grandma's garden.

That is just ridiculous. Tigers live in the jungle.
Not in the garden.

And even though there are dragonflies the size of birds
and plants that want to eat us,

and you are a **very** grumpy polar bear, there is absolutely,

definitely,
one hundred per cent no..."

"Tiger."

"Hmmm," says Nora.

"Hello,"

says the tiger.

"Um... Tigers don't live in gardens," says Nora. "Are you real?"

"I don't know," says the tiger. "Are you?"

Nora thinks about this for a long time.

"I don't know," she admits.
"How can you tell?"

"I'm not sure you can,"
says the tiger.

This makes Nora feel a bit funny.

"I have an idea," says the tiger. "If you
believe in me, then maybe I'll be real."
"And if you believe in me," says Nora,
"then maybe I'll be real too!"

"Deal?" says the tiger.
"Deal," agrees Nora.
"Come on," says the tiger.
"I'll give you a ride home."

And so Nora and Jeff ride home on the tiger's back.
They talk about breakfast, and trampolines
and the grumpy polar bear.

He really is extraordinarily friendly, for a tiger.

"Can I come and see you again?"
asks Nora, when they are near her house.
"Of course," says the tiger. "Whenever
you want me, I'll be here."

Inside, Nora and Jeff
sit down for dinner.
"There really is a tiger in the
garden, isn't there?" says Nora.
"I'm not sure," replies Grandma.
"Perhaps it's only a ginger cat.
It's hard to tell,
sometimes."

"No," says Nora, "it's
absolutely, definitely a tiger.
And do you know what?"
"What?" asks Grandma.

"There's a mermaid
in the bath."

First published in Great Britain in 2016
by Frances Lincoln Children's Books,
74-77 White Lion Street, London N1 9PF
www.franceslincoln.com

A catalogue record for this book is
available from the British Library.

ISBN 978-1-84780-806-6

Illustrated digitally

Designed by Zoë Tucker
Edited by Katie Cotton

Printed in China

9 8 7 6 5 4

For Mum, Dad and Jess, with love.